Pure Wolves

Hannah Goldberg

Contents

Prologue

Yvonne's P.O.V.

Last week was my birthday, and I'm now officially sixteen. My name is Yvonne, and I'm a werewolf. Like every werewolf, we immediately shift when we're ten. Most likely because it's when we have double digits.

Unlike the others though, I'm the Alpha's one and only child. Mom died giving birth to me, so I'm all he's got. Unfortunately, he's getting weaker and weaker because like all werewolves, we can't live without our mates. Meaning that since i'm reaching adulthood his wolf is finally starting to give out, and that I had to quickly take over the role as Alpha

So, on my birthday my dad gave his title to me as an Alpha in front of the entire pack, named the Galaxies. Sadly, for me anyways, everyone knows I haven't found my mate yet, and they're starting to get really impatient, so two weeks from now, I have to go to the 'Teasing.'

It's stupid though because it's just a huge party in Las Vegas. Well it's a party for mateless werewolves around the world. Mostly it's teenagers to early twenty mateless werewolves.

Let's get this straight, the 'Teasing' is a huge party that's held annually once a year. Meaning only mateless wolves can enter the party. Same date, same time. Though I never attended it, until now.

I never did for three reasons. First of all, my pack, and I live in Georgia. Meaning, I'd have to waste money over some stupid party, that is full of rival werewolves. Which isn't at all a good idea because we're more likely to end up in a fight with other werewolves, then find our own mate. Secondly, if I went, everyone in my pack whose mateless would follow, and that's the worst because their too overprotective when it involves me, and it drives me nuts. Let's just say that now i'm Alpha everything I have to do is multiplied by ten. Lastly, unlike everyone in my pack, I don't want a mate. At all.

Not because I'm afraid, or anything like that, but I just don't want one, so I could be an object to the guy. I hate it when guys are possessive. I have enough overprotective and crazy people in my life, I don't need my mate to be like that. I should know, I dated the neighboring pack, Alpha's son. I was thirteen at the time, and crushed on him since I was a kid, so I was happy to finally go out with him. However, later on I dumped his ass, when he tried to control me, and not let me hang out with my best friend, Donny. Anyways I don't want a mate anytime soon. If I meet him at the 'Teasing' I'd probably end up running away from him, and hide my scent for the rest of the time we'd spend there.

It pisses me off that I have to go, since the party is only for mateless wolves, Donny can't come to my rescue, he's already mated to Marisa. Donny and Marisa are my Beta's since last week. Though thankfully, my Gamma, Ryan is coming with me, along with his little sister Ashley.

Now I'm the Alpha of the Galaxies pack, the third largest, and second strongest pack in the world. Though truth be told, I'm famous. Not because of my looks, or any stupid reason like that, but because I'm the only female Alpha there is. Not only that, but I'm stronger than all the other

Alpha's in the world. In all honesty it's most likely, do to me being a 'Pure' wolf.

Pure werewolves are either fully black, or fully white. We're rare, and there's only five of us in the whole world. Only the Alpha bloodline, can be a Pure so the other four are all Alpha's, except their male.

The only thing that's different for me is that the males are white, and I'm an all black wolf. However, I'm the only black wolf in history, so I'm stronger than the white wolves. They say that when us Pure's are fully mated, and marked by our mates, we'll get powers. Like extreme out-of-this-world power But no one knows what type we will get, due to it never being recorded in history

So, I'm pretty unsure of what'll happen to me.

Anyways, a Pure is ten times faster, and stronger than a regular werewolf. We also have at least one hundred times better senses than others. Even our Alpha control is better. Meaning we don't become as out of control as other Alphas when their emotions are on overdrive.

Right now I'm counting down the days to the end of the party. At least a hundred of the mateless teens from my pack is coming to the party, thank Goddess the pack's rich. I had to buy a private plane for the whole pack, but I love them anyways, so I don't mind it much.

Though I have to thank the pack in Las Vegas because they own a huge plaza for werewolves only, and let's everyone stay for the week, so we can find our mates. That Alpha's a softie, but pretty cool.

So everyone's excited, and won't shut up about it. I love everyone in my pack, but they are so annoying this past week. Oh well. Hopefully, I don't meet my mate at the 'Teasing.' I'm just not ready. Not now. Not for a long time.

Chapter One

Yvonne's P.O.V.

My alarm went off, and I groaned sleepily. I shut it off with a smash, and I went straight to the shower.

Ten minutes later, I was fully clothed. I wore a blue v-neck, faded black skinny jeans, and black boots with heels. I put on light makeup, massacre, and dark red lipstick. As usual I put on my gold dangling earrings, a gold locket, and my charm bracelet. Then I put my long silky black hair down, which ended at my butt. I haven't cut my hair off since I was eleven, which I was proud of.

I went down stairs to see my dad multitasking, sipping his coffee, and typing something on his personal laptop on the long dining table. I see my Beta, Donny in the kitchen with my Gamma, Ryan doing who knows what. And I notice Marisa and Ashley on the couch in the living room, giggling. I smirk knowing that it was going to be fun to mess with them, and quietly sneak up on them.

Their backs to me, not realizing I'm there, i've been known to sneak up on the most alert werewolves, and it shows when they continue to giggle. "Boo!" I yelled out in a roar. They screamed like scaredy cats, and hug each other for dear life, collapsing onto the floor as they do so. Seeing them frozen in shock I laugh so hard that there were tears in my eyes. They glare at me, and trying to look serious i cover my mouth, but I end up laughing even harder.

They looked at each other, and their eyes fogged over. Their mouths go slack, and their hold on each other loosens.

Probably, mind linking each other.

After a minute, they grinned evilly at me. Instantly I feel sweat trickle down my neck, the tension in the air is suffocating, I gulp knowing what's next, and was about to run, when they tackled me in unison. I fell to the floor, both on top of me, unable to get away as they tickled me to death. Trying and trying again, yet in the end I failed to get away.

When we calmed down, Marisa crossed her arms, pouting, and told me in a pout, "Yvonne! That was mean, you scared me, I thought you were a rogue, or something!" I smirked. Marisa is sixteen, but a month older then me. She has dark blonde hair, chocolate eyes, she's 5'6, and mostly skinny. She's wearing a white hoodie, leather jeans, and leather heels.

Ashley copied Marisa's movement, and nodded at her in agreement. "Yeah, that wasn't nice." She says, glaring at me playfully. Ashley had long reddish blonde hair that fell to her hips, dark green eyes, 5'8, and freckles splattered over her face. She was a year younger than us, but we didn't care about that. She's wearing a green dress that ended at her thighs, black tights, and baby blue ballerina shoes.

I smiled, and replied shrugging, "Hey, at least you got me back." With that I walk back to the dining room. Donny hands us each a plate filled with food, and sat at the table.

Donny has curly brown hair, blue-silver eyes, 6'2, and has a strong build. He's only seventeen. He's wearing a Laker t-shirt, shorts, and sneakers.

Ryan sat next to his sister, Ashley. He has the same reddish blonde hair, but has lighter green eyes, 6'3, and he's lean. He's wearing a jacket, long pants, and blue nikes. He's sixteen, like me.

My dad begins to eat his food with his coffee. Dad has red hair, blue eyes, he's 6'7, and has wrinkles on his forehead. He's in his late forties. As usual he's wearing a fancy suit, and brown shoes.

Ten minutes later everyone's finished with breakfast, and gets ready for school. Donny kissed Marisa's forehead before heading to their room. She blushes, and I roll my eyes. Mates. "Bye, you guys. See y'all at school." I say, before slinging my backpack over my shoulder, and walking out the door.

I walk out to the garage, and open it. I walk over to my motorcycle, and put my helmet on. Both are sleek red, and still looked brand new. Yes, I do take care of Berry, (I have a habit of naming my things) he's one of my treasured things. I smile and hop on, then raced to school.

•••••••••••••LUNCHTIME•••••••••••

As per usual, I walk over to the center table in the courtyard. Every time I walked in, everyone's heads would snap to see me, and when I'd stare back they'd bow their heads back in submission.

My friends wave me over, and I nod at them. I walk over, and sit next to Jayleen, my cousin from my dad's side. She has red hair that's pulled in a pony tail, soft brown eyes, 5'7, and is thin. She's wearing a black crop top, a black undershirt, blue booty shorts, and dark blue heels that matched.

She's the same age as, Ashley, and their like sisters. "Alpha, are you ready for the "Teasing?' Today's Friday, so that means we're going tonight. What time do we come?" Jayleen asks, bowing her head in submission.

I nod, and face everyone at my table. In my Alpha tone, I say, "Trays off, and move." They bow their heads and walk off to other tables, to sit.

I jump in the air, and onto the table. I clear my throat, and give a loud whistle that echoes around the area. Everyone goes silent, and turn to stare at me. "Everyone! Can you hear me?" I ask loudly.

I hear a choruses of 'yes' and 'yes, Alpha' everywhere. I smile, and put my hand to my hip. Thank Goddess that dad made a high school only for Werewolves, even some of the neighboring packs go here, along with a few rogues. My dad taught everyone that we need to accept everyone, no matter if it's our greatest enemy, or a lone rogue, who doesn't have it's own pack.

"Listen up. As you all know. Today we're going to Las Vegas for the 'Teasing.' Though it's the first time this pack is going, you know that if you find your mate, and have to join that pack, you must inform me. I know it's sad that some of us will leave, and probably never again will we see each other, but remember you are always welcome back. And also I love you guys, without a doubt. I wish we had more time together, but we're all family, and don't you forget it. I've already asked the principal, for permission if everyone can leave after lunch, and hang out in the field for the rest of the day. Which he granted. So everyone please come visit me, so we can say our goodbyes. Come to the pack house at eight o'clock sharp. You may go back to your eating." I said, wiping a tear that escaped my eye. Then I hopped off the table, and motioned my group back. Everyone began to clap, scream joyfully, and come over to hug me.

I knew that everyone needed that because I felt everyone's sadness throughout the morning, especially mine. Even my wolf, Grace whimpered the entire day.

I looked around the area, to see the girls in tears, and the guys with glossy eyes. I couldn't take it any longer, so I shouted in my Alpha voice, "Everyone, come here for a family hug!"

For the rest of the school hours, we cried and hugged. I'm scared, that everyone would leave, and that they'd never come back.

Yvonne, it's what's destined for us. We'll still have the guys, only the girls who find their mates, have to move., Grace said positively.

That doesn't make it better, Grace. All of them are my family. Their the missing piece, to my puzzle.We will never be able to replace the girls. Not now, not ever., I shot back at her.

I hear Grace sigh. I know, I know, I'll miss them too, but you're making them feel worse than they already are. Anyways what about us? The 'Teasing' might have our mates there, Grace mumbles.

Mates? Grace, don't you mean mate?, I ask.

Uhhh.... Yeah. You wouldn't understand it, even if I told you, Grace said quietly.

Hmmm, I say.

She probably, meant him, and his wolf, I think.

••••••AFTER SCHOOL(AT HOME)•••••

After school I headed home. Well, not exactly. My house is actually, the pack house. Only the the Alpha, Beta, Gamma, and Delta families live in the pack house. Everyone else lives around the neighborhood. Even the Warriors don't live in the pack house, but they do live right next to us in any case of emergency.

Like I said, it's good to be rich because without that, we couldn't provide stuff for the pack. Though it's mostly a small part of the government who are werewolves, and a few humans sworn to secrecy, that provide money to all packs. However those who are werewolves that work in the government, must be rogues because if they have a pack then others will say their taking advantage of the power, and whatnot.

As I walk into the pack house, I hear yelling. A lot of yelling. Like every good Alpha, I come running into the kitchen to see what the problem is.

There in the kitchen is, my Delta and best friend screaming at each other. And guess what? Their in the middle of a fire, in the freakin' kitchen! Alex is shouting, and splashing water all over the stove, where the fire is. While Julie is using the fire extinguisher. Then the fire soon dies out, and now stood a big white soapy mess in the kitchen.

"WHAT THE HELL, IS GOING ON?!" I scream in my Alpha voice. Their faces pale, and then bow their heads in submission. They stay silent, but look at each other. Mind linking. "I ASKED YOU A QUESTION! ANSWER, NOW." I said in an angry tone.

Julie looks at me, and gives me a small hesitant smile. She has short brown hair, green speckled eyes, 5'4, and is light weight. She's wearing a blue summer dress that's now covered in white foam, and has black sandals on. She's sixteen, obviously. "Sorry, Alpha. I came in here a minute or two ago and the whole place was in flames... So I used the fire extinguisher. You have to ask Alex, what happened." Julie explains, gesturing to the blackened counter.

I soften, a little, and nod. "Tell me." I demand calmly, but in Alpha voice..

Alex looks at the ground, and plays with his hands. Alex has red hair, bluish brown eyes, about 6'2, and has a six pack. He's wearing a plain white shirt, and jeans, no shoes. He's eighteen. "Well... Like you said it's our last day with everyone, so I wanted to make a couple of cakes for everyone, while we're on the plane. But as you can see that didn't turn out, um... Good." He tells us.

I sigh heavily. "Clean it up. While we're gone, I want you to hire people to redesign the whole kitchen. For now, just clean it up." I say and walk out of the kitchen.

This is going to be a long weekend. Isn't it, Grace?, I ask her.

Yup. You know it. I can't wait to go to the 'Teasing', Grace squeals.

I groan, but tell her, I guess we just have to wait, and see.

I can feel her nod, and then yawns. Night, Yvonne, she says.

I yawn too, and say, Goodnight, Gracie.

Then I fall asleep, and give in to the darkness.

Chapter Two

Yvonne's P.O.V

Hours passed by, and we finally arrived at Las Vegas. I checked my watch, only to see that it was only five o'clock in the morning. I ushered the pack out of the plane, all pack members who ranged from the age thirteen to others in their early twenties.

Let me explain why there are only the younger werewolves here. First off, when werewolves turn thirteen, that's when our body goes through maturity, that makes us able to shift into a wolf, also to be able to communicate to our wolves, and that's the age when we're able to find or search our mates. However, if they are younger than you by months, or years, you cannot locate them till they mature also. Which can prove frustrating when you're wolf's instincts are to find, and mate with them.

Anyways, there are, a hundred seventy three pack members that came along with me, meaning that I had to get eleven long limos to fit everyone.

A man with black hair, brown eyes, 5'11, and a strong chin stood in front of all the limos. He wore an expensive gray suit, and black shoes. He was probably in his late thirties. He walked over to me, and bowed, showing respect to my pack and I. "My name's Charlie, I'm the Beta for Equality pack." Charlie said, easily shaking my hand, his grip firm.

I smiled politely, and said, "I am Yvonne, Alpha of Galaxies pack."

After introductions, we entered our limos, and drove off. Charlie stayed with my group, to explain some things. "As you know, the party lasts to six till the next day. Our hotel let's everyone stay here for the weekend until Monday. This will give everyone time to transition to new packs. Oh, and the party will be on the top floor, and rooftop." Charlie explained.

I nodded as I listened, keeping an open mind link to everyone,so that they heard his explanation too. I felt everyone's bubbling excitement, and they all said 'Yes!' when he finished speaking, I asked if they all got what he explained.

••••••AT THE EQUALITY'S PLAZA•••••

I made sure that everyone settled into their rooms, and I quickly fell asleep as soon as I hit the bed. Since it was only six now, I told the pack to go to sleep, so that they could get some rest, until we had to go and get ready for the Teasing.

______FOUR HOURS LATER______

It was 10:13 when my friends came squealing in, and told me to come to breakfast. Thus, made me yell at them to go away, or else, and I quickly went back to sleep, ignoring their yells. Let's just say I'm not a morning person.

Anyways, my pack had floors seven, eight, and nine. So we decided to meet in the casino for breakfast, which was on the eighth floor. I let my hair down, curling it into ringlets at the bottom. I dressed up in my black leather jacket, purple v-neck, matching black leather pants, and black heeled boots. I put dark blue mascara that helped my ivory green eyes pop, and some pinkish red lipstick.

As I entered the casino, all eyes were on me. Even other packs that came watched me. My pack, of course, ate it up, and wolf whistled at me. I smirk, and walk over to them, gracefully.

Jayleen, Ashley, Ryan, Alex, and Julie sat at the center table of the food court, in the casino. Julie waved me over, happily. "Alpha! You're up!" Julie said, as I sat on the chair, next to her.

"No thanks to you guys." I grumbled.

They laugh at me, while Alex looks at me innocently. "Whatcha, talking about? We've been here the whole time." He said.

I shook my head, and glared at him. "Right. That's SO true." I told him sarcastically.

I notice another pack come in, and I smell hazelnuts, and lavender. I immediately hide my scent, and excuse myself to the bathroom. As I walk away, I notice a guy around my age sniff the air. He had black and blonde hair, hazel blue eyes, about 6'3, and had plump, kissable lips.

Grace, is howling, and yelling at me to go to him now.

Mate! Go to him now. He's ours. His wolf is asking where we are. I WANT HIM, NOW!, Grace whined at me.

No! I don't want a mate, not now. Let's go back to our friends, I say to her.

Fine, Grace says, pouting.

I wait for a minute, and stand there, then as I turn around and walk back to my table, I see the guy from earlier looking at me curiously, before walking away. I sigh in relief, and think, This is gonna be a long weekend.

Chapter Three

C hapter 3:

Re-Edited

Ash's P.O.V.

Some of my pack members, and I decided to have breakfast in the food court that's in the casino. Though most stayed in their rooms to dress up, and get ready for the ceremony.

As I walked into the floor, my pack on both sides of me, in a protective half circle, I was chatting with Elli, my little sister.

Elli had red hair that's curly at the ends, light blue eyes, 5'4, and is curvy. She's fifteen. Right now she's wearing a red top, skinny jeans, and white flip flops.

Then it hit me, a strong alluring scent. It smelled like peaches, and raspberries. My wolf howled in content, and love. I looked everywhere, but as soon as the scent came, it vanished.

My wolf, Sam growled, angrily.

What's wrong, Sam?, I asked confused.

She's, our mate... We found her... That's why that scent lured you in, but... SHE HID HER SCENT, SO WE CANNOT FIND HER!, Sam whimpered, both sad and angry.

Doesn't that mean she's mates with, Brad, and Connor too?, I ask, happily.

Yes, but only because you're all identical, not fraternal triplets. However now we have to find her. It seems that she doesn't want to be found at the moment, so be sure to pay attention to everything. Remember we can still find her if we touch her. So tell our brothers, she's playing hide and seek. They'll find her., Sam replies.

Ok, I said.

I mind linked my two brothers, who are my triplet siblings. We're only seventeen. All three of us are the Alpha's of the Moonless pack. The largest, and strongest pack in the world. Our territory is in a secluded area in the U.S.

Anyways, my brother's, and I are very special. Not only are we triplet Alphas, which is one of a kind, We're Pure wolves.

As you know there's only five of us in the whole world. So my brother's and I are all white, but we have different eye colors. Brad has burgundy-blue eyes, while Conner has silver-green eyes, and I have golden-red eyes.

We're not the strongest Alpha's though, nor are we the strongest Pure's, it is however, the only female Alpha, not only is she that first female Alpha in history, she's also the first female Pure. Though unmated, she's still stronger than any Alpha in the world. Unlike us, she's all black, only her pack, the Galaxies pack, has ever seen her wolf. So many believe she's a myth, or at least a terrible beast, that cares for no one, but her pack. She's ten times stronger than Pure white wolves. Not even my brothers and I could take her on, even if we attacked her at the same time, most likely we'd all lose in a matter of seconds.

She's supposedly won against all the Alphas at age ten, ranking her the strongest Alpha in the world. My brother's, and I were out that day, so we couldn't see how she beat our dad. Even now, my dad still has yet to tell us what she did, in order to beat him because the only witnesses to this event was our mother whom was the Luna of the pack before we took over, the Beta, Delta, and Gamma. Of course loyal to our father, will not tell us either.

Anyways, I heard that her packs came for the Teasing for the first time. Some said it's because their elders are putting pressure on her, to find her mate. Though she'll stay as the Alpha, she still needs to have her mate, so she will be recognized officially as the Alpha to her pack.

Brad! Conner! I've smelt our mate earlier, but Sam said she hid her scent. So keep an eye out for her. I'm on floor eight, so most likely she's from the Galaxies pack., I warned them, through mind link.

What?! She hid her scent!? Why?, Conner's wolf, Liam whimpered.

I shrugged through mind link, and said, Dunno. Just find her!

Ok, fine..., Brad says.

See ya, later bro. I'm with Amy, right now. So I'm gonna play with her for awhile. I don't want a mate, so I'm staying out of this., Conner says smugly.

Ugh. Amy's the pack slut, and would do anything to get fucked. She came onto Brad, and I before, not to mention she tried to fully mate with Conner once. Conner's an idiot, he may be an Alpha, but he doesn't want a mate. He's famous for being the 'bad boy' in school. Connor, and Amy have an off-again-on-again relationship. Right now their on, and dating. If that's what you call it. I sigh in frustration.

Whatever, Conner. She's our mate, you're supposed to love her, and take care of her! I just told you the situation, but you don't give a fuck! Liam wants her, probably you do too, but you're being such an ass!

Who cares! Leave me alone!, Conner roars, and cuts off the link.

It's fine, Ash. I'll help you look. You know how Connor feels., Brad says.

Okay. See you tonight. I'm gonna go eat. Bye., I said calmly, and tune out of the link.

I notice a cute girl staring at me. She has long black hair, that curled, ivory green eyes, 6'2, and totally sexy. She's wearing a black leather jacket, purple v-neck, matching black leather pants, and black heeled boots. She has dark blue mascara that make her eyes pop, and some pinkish red lipstick.

She looked hot, I could feel power, stronger than mine, radiate from her. I turn away from her, knowing if I looked at her any longer I'd submit to her. I knew right away who she was, she was the Pure black wolf, number one Alpha, throughout the world.

For some reason my wolf whined and growled at me. I thought maybe she might be my mate... But I shook it off. The hottest and strongest she-wolf as our mate? Yea, right!

I feel Sam pace inside my head, and growl at me.

What's wrong with you?, I ask.

Wait and see., he says, growling.

Ok..., I said, then shut off our connection.

This is going to be a weird week, I think to myself, and walk towards my pack.

Chapter Four

Yvonne's P.O.V.

Right now, the girls and I are in my hotel room, getting ready for the party. Which, sadly starts in hour starts in half an hour. Meaning I have to be prepared to avoid all male wolves, that aren't in my pack for as long as possible, till the end of the party. All the Alpha's that are at the party have to meet up ten minutes early, though, so we can get to the stage, and introduce our pack. Meaning I'll be surrounded by overbearing male wolves.

I left my room, heading to the top floor that also has the roof. I wore a red silk dress to the floor, a gold clutch, black pumps, a necklace, gold-silver dangling earrings, and a charm bracelet. I wore light make up, mascara, red lipstick, and eyeshadow.

I entered the building, and felt the room radiate with power. The scent of Alpha dominance, wafted in the air, it could've been suffocating for a normal wolf, who would have to submit the second they stepped into the room. As I walk in the room it fell silent, and everyone looked at me. There eyes roamed my body, and their wolves urging them to submit. In the room stood eleven young, and very hot men in here.

"Hello. Greetings to you, Alphas. As you know, I am Yvonne, Alpha of the Galaxies pack. Who, may I ask, are you?" I asked with power in my calm voice. They all looked at me, but not meeting my eyes, the air of dominance, quickly changed to submission.

A man in his twenties, stepped forward, he smiled at me, trying to be nice. He had spiked up brown hair, hard brown eyes, chiseled jaw, and is about 5'10. He wore a colored vest, jeans, and sneakers. "Hello, Alpha Yvonne. I'm Jonathan, the Alpha of the Emerald pack. The second largest, and third strongest. Nice to meet you." Jonathan said, holding his hand out. I take it, and shake it. His face flushes when I touch him, his wolf seemed to scream hormones, and submission all at once.

"Hi, I'm Brad. I'm Alpha of the Moonless pack, along with my two brothers." Brad said holding his hand out. He had black hair, icy blue eyes, about 6'2, and had full pink, kissable lips. I, of course, didn't think twice, and grabbed it. My whole body tingled, practically shivered in happiness, and my wolf howled.

I stood there frozen, everyone else looking at me in shock. They had obviously seen the mating bong connect, I could smell it, feel it in the air, "So you're our mate? Ash said you were hiding from us." A boy with blonde hair, teal blue eyes, about 6'3, and kissable lips said. I stood there frozen. "I'm Conner by the way, and that's Ash." he said to me, and pointed to the first triplet I saw and smelled. They all looked at me hungrily, their wolves we're dominating the room with lust, and love so much, it was hard to tell apart the emotions.

"You should bring your scent back, it can't help you now." Ash said smirking, then he began stalking towards me. His body seemed to glide as he came towards me, my wolf buzzing in excitement, as Connor continued to hold my arm, his grip on me was soft, but firm. His touch sent sparks, and tingles throughout my body.

Of course, the first reasonable thing I did was, flip the mate that was man handling me, and run for it. Yeah, i'm not a really reasonable person.

I looked back, and saw the triplets shocked, hurt, and angry faces that stared right at me, their gazes were unflinching. It scared the crap out of me.

You shouldn't have done that., Grace tells me, in a calm, sweet voice.

Whatever. UGH! I can't believe I have three mates!, I shout at her.

I feel her shrug at me, and she howled happily. Finally, I get my mates! And their, let me spell it out for you: H.O.T!, she yelps, which quickly turns into a lustful howl.

I cut the connection with her, with an irritated huff, and continue running.

!

Chapter Five

Connor's P.O.V.

What the hell?! That bitch fucking flipped me over, like it was nothing! I mean come on, I probably weigh twice as more than she does. This is fucking ridiculous! When I get her, I swear, she's gonna regret it.

My brothers and I were chasing after her, but she was way faster than us. Though, I guess it makes sense since she's the only Pure black wolf. But still, I mean we were using our full on speed, which i'm hoping that means she was too, if not there's no freaking way we're gonna get close to her. Not at all.

She went into the elevator ten feet in front of us, and as it began to close she smirked. Then she shouted, "See ya guys later! Try, and find me! If you can, that is!" She tossed her hair back, winks at us, of course she rubs it in our faces when she throws her head back, and laughs at us, then with that the elevator closed.

We stand there panting, too out of breath to move. We stay like that in silence for a moment, that seems to pass slowly by.

"Well... At least we know who are mate is. Ash, what should we do? She still has her scent closed off from us, and there's twenty five floors in this damn hotel, not to mention there's like seventy rooms on all the floors. She could be literally anywhere. Or she might not even be here in the hotel anymore, considering how fast she can run, i'm assuming she's already long gone." Brad finally says, breaking the silence.

"Well, we need to go to her pack first. We'll tell them we're her mates, and ask where'd she go.They'll tell us if we ask nice enough." Ash suggested.

I thought about it. At first I didn't want a mate... But now I wanted her. Badly. I love her already, and her personality. Even if she is stronger, and flipped me over. I'll show her who's boss, anyways. All three of us will. She'll fall to our feet, and beg us for more.

"I'm coming too." I told them.

Ash smirked knowingly, and Brad stared at me coldly. "You can. But first off break it off with Amy. I swear, if you play around, now that we have a mate, I'll fucking kill you." Brad threatened.

I nod, and said, "Ok. Wait and give me a minute."

Then I mindlink Amy. Amy, you there? We need to talk., I said.

Hey, baby. What's up? Do you want a quickie in my room?, Amy purrs.

No. My brothers, and I found our mate., I tell her, my voice polite, and pity-filled.

So? Just reject her. She's probably a slut. I'm your girlfriend, anyways., Amy says irritated.

I growl at her. SHUT UP! I wanted to talk to you because I want to break up with you. She's my mate. Not you., I growl out at her.

She whimpers . Yes, Alpha., She says defeatedly.

Good., I say, and cut off the connection.

I come back to reality, to see my brother's waiting for me at the elevator. "Hurry up! Let's go! I want to claim our mate now." Ash demands.

"Coming!" I yell, and race over. We walk into the elevator, and I ask, "So where are we going?"

Brad cuts in, before Ash says anything, "We're going to the roof, that's where the packs have to be introduced. Remember? The Alpha that hosts the party points out which pack, is which. Though, of course he's the only Alpha that can come to the Teasing when he already has a mate, because it's his hotel, and territory."

I groan, but nod. "Great there's at least thirty packs here. It'll take forever! I mean come on, we don't know who's in her pack, so we have to wait forever." I say.

"Not really. He goes by rank on the largest packs to the least, so we won't have to wait for long." Ash says, checking his phone. He continues, "We're a few minutes late, so he's probably done with the annual speech, and is introducing our pack."

I sigh, and the elevator door opens. We step out, and look around the area. Everyone goes silent, and stares at us, the Alpha on the stage, George, waves at us.

Then he clears his throat, and when everyone's gazes turn back to him, he continues, "This is the first time ever since the third largest, and second strongest pack, the Galaxies have came here. Here they are!" He points to a large group of good looking people. The spot light drifts towards them, and they all wave. They all are dresses fancy, their scent gives off pine, and lavender. Every pack gives off the scent of their territory, so you can distinctly tell what pack their in.

Ash, Brad, and I share a look. We nod, and walk over towards them.

Ash takes the lead, and walks over to the and shouts at them, "Hey!"

A guy around our age, walks in front of the pack. He has reddish blonde hair, light green eyes, 6'3, and he's lean. He has power radiate from him, not enough to be a Beta, so he's probably the Gamma of the pack. "Yes? What do you want, Alpha...?" He asks.

"Ash. That's Brad, and Connor. We're your Alpha's mates, and she ran away from us. Where is she?" Ash says bluntly.

The group starts to whisper, but don't look surprised. The guy turns and glares at them. They all go silent when he holds a hand up to silence them. "Well, I don't know. She didn't say anything to us, so that means she's probably hiding in the game room. She spent most of the day in there because the Alpha who runs the place locked it up, and gave her the key to it, for her use only. So she'll be there. Oh, by the way Alpha's i'm the Gamma, Ryan. Good luck, you'll need it." Ryan says, then snaps his finger at his pack, and they turn their back to us, focussing on the Alpha, who's still speaking on the stage, and introducing other packs.

We jog back towards the elevator and head to the game room. Which is on floor twenty, and takes up one half of the floor.

"This will be fun." I say dirtily.

"You know it." My brothers reply back to me in unison, as we walk over to the door that had bolded letters on it: GAME ROOM.

The next thing I know, all three of us kick the door open at the same time, with all our force. The door burst open, with a crack, and flies out into the room to land on top of a hockey table. From a few feet away, I see our beautiful mate, look at us in shock.

I smirk at her, and think, Oh, how she will regret running away from us.

****

SO? How do you like it so far? In the next chapter I have a few ideas that y'all might enjoy. Anyways, do you like Conner's POV? I'll do Brad's POV soon.

Also please comment, vote, tell your followers, add it to ur reading list, and follow me!!!!

Umm... Check out Why I Ran by _Grace_Carroll_. As I've mentioned on Surviving Terror, I'm co-authoring on the new story she's going to write. But check her story out you'll like it & follow her too.

I have one tiny little favor for everyone... Please read my other stories. Surviving Terror, Find Me, and the rest. Please I need every thing I'm writing to be out there.

Thanks. So far this story has the most views, BUT I want my others to have similar out comes. So please check them out.

Anyways... I was wondering who'd like to co author on a story I just posted: Find Me.

Summary for this one:

Carson charter high school:A boarding school filled with boys.

One day the principal announces that that they will have a contest.That a girl is hidden here for one whole year.If they figure out who she is,and reveals it, the guys get a huge party and have A's for the whole year.Howe ver, if the girl's identity is secret for one year,girls can come to the boarding school,and she will become the principal.

At first the boys think it'll be easy, but the rules are hectic.#1:You can't take off the freshman's clothes.#2:You can't look through their personal belon gings.#3:You must work in groups of 5 or more to be allowed to reveal who she is.#4:You must have full proof of who she is, by having a picture of her as a girl,true name,DNA,and status.#5:She may have doubles throughout the school and friends who can protect her, if needed.

Each month, the girl must give a hint to who she is but not reveal it.New year starts,and high school is just the beginning.Who's the girl&Will she be found?

Or another story I'm thinking about writing. The story for this one is called: The Gang Leader, And The Advice-Giving Nerd__________________

Here's the summary:

"Be my girlfriend for 6 months, if you do I won't tell everyone your VALENTINE." He smirks down at me, and plays with my hair, then he continues, "However, if you fall in love with me, in these 6 months, I'll take your everything. If you don't then I'll let you do whatever you want me to for a whole year. Does that sound fair?"

*

Faith Cupid, 16, is a girl who's parents are dead, and is now living with her god mother. In school she's known as the hot but loner nerd, who only speaks to Lance and the teachers. However out of school, she's the famous internet sensation: VALENTINE. A girl who has Kik, website, Twitter, Meow, Facebook, & Instagram, that millions of people go to to get advice on life. Everyone knows about her, but they don't know who she is. They all try, but fail because do to inherited money, all the devices she uses are untraceable.

One day she gets a text from "Secret_Rover" this guy won't stop texting her, yet a week later she finds out who he is: Michael Vance age 15.

Chapter Six

✱ Edited*Yvonne's P.O.V.

So here I am, staring at my hot triplet mates, utterly shocked. In the middle of the game room, in front of the ski ball game.

How the heck did they know I was here?!, I think.

Probably from our pack mates. That's the most logical answer. Duh!, Grace answers me.

Shut up!, I yell at her.

Hey, don't get your panties in a twist, alright? Have fun with the guys, I'm leaving now, 'cause this ain't gonna be pretty., Grace says before shutting me out.

I sigh, and look at my mates again. Man, do they look pissed, and a little sad. I feel guilty for a second, but wave the thought away.

"So, our little mate, do you want it the easy way, or the hard way?" Brad said seductively.

My wolf howled with joy, as I shivered at his voice. But then I put an emotionless mask on, showing I wasn't afraid. A dirty thought went through my mind, and I smirked.

Oh, hell no! Yvonne, I swear if you do that I'll kill you!, Grace said.

I laugh, and tell her, Whatever. Just so you know, you can't kill me, 'cause technically we're the same person. Duh!

You know, what I mean., Grace sighs, frustrated.

Smirking I play with my red dress. "I wonder what I look like with my lingerie. Oh wait, I already do. But do you guys know?" I question, sexily, and tug down the sleeves to reveal my bare shoulders.

My mates eyes burn holes through my body, and I hear them pant. I smirk, wider. I walk slowly to them, making their little guys pop up with anticipation. I slowly take off my beautiful heels, and stop. "Do you want me?" I ask huskily.

"Oh, goddess, yes." They say in unison, voices raw.

I take two slow steps to them, six feet in front of them. "Do you need me?" I ask them in the same tone.

"Y-Yes!" Brad stutters.

I start to take my dress, and hear the boys growl, wanting. As I fully take off my dress, I grab my heels, and step forward. They don't pay much attention as I zip past them, and stand next to the door. Probably because I'm wearing VICTORIA SECRET black and white lingerie. "Then, come, and get me boys. After all you are my MATES." I tell them smirking, then I shift into my black wolf, and run out of the game room. Holding my dress, and heels in my mouth.

Not again! That's so unfair!, Grace shouts at me.

Too bad! Whether you like it, or not I'm the strongest there is, and I'm gonna teach them that they have to love me as me, not because of touch, and smell., I tell her.

I hear her sigh, but nod.

Ok. I get it. Have it your way, Yvonne. They'll find you eventually., Grace says, and shuts me out.

Chapter Seven

As I ran down the halls to level eight, I bumped into some one. I was still in my wolf form, so I looked down, and saw I bumped a girl my age down.

She looked up at me, in awe, and submitted to me in seconds. I gave her a wolfish smile and look around. No one was here except for us, so I transformed back, and put on my dress. "Hi. My names Yvonne, the Alpha of the Galaxies pack. You are?" I ask.

"I-I'm Alice Summers, the Warriors daughter of Emerald pack. Nice to meet you Alpha." She says, and bows her head. Summer was very pretty, white silver blonde hair, bright blue eyes, 5'10, and skinny, but muscular. She wore a lip ring, a black skull chocker, black v neck, faded black leather jacket, black skinny jeans, and black stiletto heels.

"Your so pretty. Come on, I'm hiding from my mates, right now. Come with me!" I tell her, and drag her with me to the top floor, which was the roof.

"Mates?" Alice asks, surprised.

I smile. "Yeah, their Alpha's of the Moonless pack. Ash, Brad, and Conner, their all bloody hot!" I shout.

She giggles, and says, "Lucky! Anyways, I'm sixteen, how old are you?"

"Same, I'll introduce you to my pack. I have this feeling..." I mumble the last part.

It was true, I did have this feeling, about this pretty girl.

Hmmm... It's your powers that's kicking in., Grace says.

Probably because I met my mates, right?, I ask her.

Yeah, maybe., Grace replies.

Ok. I'll talk to you later., I say, as Alice and I walk out the elevator.

Ok, bye., Grace says before cutting me off.

"Come on! Smell! Do you think your mates here?" I ask her, my instincts kicking in.

She looks at me confused, before putting her nose in the air, and sniffing. She looks surprised, and smiles at me. When she says that one simple word, I know that my powers are coming soon, "Yes."

I notice my Gamma, coming up behind her, and says, "Hello, mate."

That's when I smile, and walk away, to tell my pack the news.

Chapter Eight

✳ Edited*Brad's P.O.V.

JEEZ... This is gonna be a long day... My brothers, and I go to the roof, to check our pack. I walk out the elevator, and immediately spot our little mate, dancing alone. All eyes on her.

My brothers, and I growl when the all the guys who stared at her hungrily. Yvonne looks at us with a sweet smile, and beckons is to her. Slowly Everyone turns to us, and gasps.

We pay no attention to them, as we walk over to our sexy mate. When we reach her, I dance behind her, my hands circling her upper thighs, not caring that the crowd is watching. I feel her shiver, and her breath hitch.

I notice Ash dancing next to her, on the right. He's grinding on her lower thigh, making her pant. I smell Yvonne's scent, peaches and raspberries, which she released just now.

My wolf growls, and purrs. I look around to see all the guys eyes black with desire, do to Yvonne's arousal. The three of us growl in unison, making them look down, submissively.

In front of Yvonne is Conner. His hand are on her waist, clutching her hard, as he sucks her sweet spot where he'll mark her. Which is behind her left ear, where her jaw, and neck meet. I hear her whimper, and moan, sexily. Her hand roaming his chest.

"Wait.... Aaaaaaahhhhh..... Wait, Conner!" Yvonne says, as he sucks harder. I can smell her arousel grow stronger, and notice she's squeezing her legs together. I smirk.

Conner finally gets off her, and gives her a sly smirk. He noticed it too. "Can we mark you?" Ash asks her, giving her a peck on the lips.

She blushes slightly, and nods. "Yes. But can I have all of you now?" She asks.

All our eyes go to a dark black, and in a husky voice we reply, "Yes, our little mate. Let us eat you."

I see her eyes go dark, she smirks, and walks to the elevator. We follow behind. All our wolves growling in need.

****

! sorry if it's short, but this is how I wanted it to end.

Chapter Nine

My mates, and I are practically running to their room. Though I'm behind them, so I know were I'm going.

Finally! Goddess, I totally love you! We got THREE HOT MATES!, Grace purred happily.

I smiled at her, and said, Yup three guys... And right now I get to have them.

All of them!, Grace continued to purr.

I was about to reply, when my mates stopped at a door, that was painted gold, and white.

They turn to look at me, gazes questioning. I smile, and purr lovingly at them, which they respond to. Ash turns back to the door, and unlocks it. Brad hugs me from behind, and nibbles at my right ear. While Conner, stands in front of me, and gives me a quick passionate kiss.

Ash opens the door, and enters. Followed by Brad, and Conner. They all sit down on the bed, as I look around the room. Three beds, that they moved to make it a large bed, a couch, three desks, windows, and other things I didn't care to notice.

I look behind me one more time. I know that when I close the door, right then, is that I'm about to lose my virginity. Not only that, but I was about to be marked- no, claimed by THREE 'PURE' ALPHAS.

****

Chapter Ten

I slowly walk torwards them, my heart beating a thousand miles a minute. Their eyes, dark with love and lust. I wonder if i'm ready...

Yes, we both are! They wont hurt us! Our mates love us. Both the wolves, and the humans care about us, equally! They are our loves, Grace howls in frustration.

I sigh, Yeah your right. Ok, i'm ready., I tell her.

Good, cause look!, Grace shouts before cutting me off.

I look at my mates to see them, surrounding me. I walk towards Ash, since he's the first born, and tug at his shirt. He smiles, and bends down. He kisses me hotly, our lips battling, he bites my bottom lip, and sucks it. I moan, opening my mouth wholly. His tongue taste enters my mouth, the sensation makes me moan, and I break the kiss to breath.

Ash slowly moves to the crook of my neck on the right, and leaves a trail of slow burning kisses until he reached his mark. Which was the base of my neck meet my shoulder on the right. He slowly looked at me, his hazel blue eyes, a dark blackish blue. Not breaking contact he lick his spot, I shiver, and plead him with my eyes. He smirks, and gives a slow lick all over the spot. Then I moan, and arch my head back, as I whisper, "Please!"

He gives in, and slowly elongates his fang on the spot. I scream in pain and pleasure. Panting, I go to the crook of his neck on the same spot, I begin to suck hard, and Ash groans, grabbing my ass. I elongate my fang, and mark him. He groans again, and pulls me close. I giggle, and give him a peck on the lips.

I take off my heels, and dress. Leaving me in my lingerie, my panties soaking. I walk slowly to Brad, the second oldest of my mates.

As I breath, he places his lips above my breasts, in the middle, and sinks his tooth into me. I shout lovingly, "More!" He sinks his tooth in deeper, and my moan increases. Brad let's go, and takes his shirt off. I go to the same spot, and lick it. He was half way in his groan when I put my tooth on the spot, and penetrate the skin. He shouts in pain, that quickly turns to pleasure.

I get off him, and look at Conner, who's watching me with anticipation, on his desk. I put my hair down, and take my bra off. I point at him, and do a hand motion, saying, "Come."

He obeys, and takes control. He grabs my waist roughly, and pulls me down to the bed.

He goes back to his spot on the left from before, and quickly sinks his fang down, as his left hand squeezes my right breast, rubbing it.

I pant, and pull him to me. I mark him, in the same place he did me, he cries out in pleasure, and I smile. Then I look over to Ash, and Brad, and say, "Strip, because I'm having all of you now."

Chapter Twelve

✱ Edited*Yvonne's P.O.V.

I woke up, to find arms wrapped around my body.

Ash was on the right, his arms around my waist. His face angelic.

Where as, I smiled at his cuteness, Brad was on my stomach sleeping soundly. Though, I don't know how he can sleep with the covers over his face.

As for Conner, he was on my left, both arms around my boobs. Perv.

I started, to untangle myself when, all three of my mates, growled sleepily, and in unison said, "Stay, and sleep Yvonne."

I don't know how the hell they do that, I thought to myself.

Well, maybe... Actually I dunno. Guess it's a triplet thing, Grace replies.

I roll my eyes, and say, it's like they practice it though.

Totally true, Grace says with an amused growl.

I turn to face the guys, and say, "We're Alphas, and we need to check on our packs, duh."

The again, in unison reply, "Nooooooo........."

I giggle and say, "Come on I know your hungry."

Brad smiles mischievously at me, and says, "Ok then, only if you kiss me first."

I blush, but then return his mischievous smile, and peck him on the lips. Not without seductively licking his lips of course.

With that, I run into the bathroom and I turn around to see my other mates laughing hysterically, and Brad shocked. I wink at them, not bothering to hide my bare body, and tell them, "I'm going to my hotel room later, and to get ready. Now let me pee and get dressed, so you guys can dress up. I'll see you at the Buffet later."

-------TWENTY MINUTES LATER-----I was walking out of my room, in my favorite outfit. I wore a black chocker with silver spikes, a black lip ring witch was chained with my right black earring on the top of my ear, a leather back crop jacket, a purple v-neck that was tight in the right places also revealing my belly which had a black belly piercing, dark blue jeans, and black and purple pumps.

My makeup was simple, mascara, eye liner, and dark red lipstick.

As I walk to the buffet from yesterday, I notice whispers of other wolves:

"...who would've thought she'd be those guys' mates..."

"...and here I thought I'd get some fun with those three..."

"...damn lucky guys. Do you realize how hot she is? I..."

"...Yes!!! I called it, I knew she'd mate them..."

"...I wonder if they'll combine both packs..."

"...I bet she'll get pregnant in no time..."

I ignore their stares and go to were my pack is, only to realize that different wolves were in the table with them, the tables combined.

I notice my mates there, smirking at me, and mouthing, creepily in unison, 'Took you long enough.'

I see some of the wolves from their pack holding hands with most of my friends.

They all look at me knowingly, and I notice Julie looks at me with a scowl. I can tell I'm in deep shit, but I shrug.

She narrows her eyes at me, and says to me via mind link, You have some explaining to do.

Okay, okay. I tell you later okay?, I tell her.

Damn straight, I love ya, but I wanna know everything. Got it?, She says in a growl.

I smile, and reply, Yup.

Well let the fun begin, I thought to myself.

Chapter Thirteen

 Edited*Yvonne's P.O.V.

I sat down at my seat that was across my mates. Julie was to my right and my Gamma, Ryan was to my left, holding hands with Alice who was next to him.

I noticed Jayleen, Ashley, and Alex are holding hands with their mates.

I smile and look over at them, I ask, "Are you gonna introduce them to me? Name, pack, and age."

Jayleen giggles happily, and says, "This is Danny, he's the Beta of your mates pack."

Danny has light brown hair, sparkling green eyes, 6'2, and a nice build. He wore a black jacket, a snap back, jeans, and Nikes.

Danny says, "I'm nineteen, nice to meet you Alpha... Or is it Luna now?"

"Alpha cause I'm still stronger than my mates." I reply, as my mates shrug.

Ashley smiles at me with joy, but sadness also, and says, "Well, this is my mate Joshua, he's from the Emerald pack... The Beta... So I have to leave..."

Tears form in all our eyes, and we become silent. Joshua has light reddish brown hair, brown eyes, 6'1, and has stubble on his chin. He wore a Nike shirt, black pants, a ring on his thumb, and sneakers.

Joshua clears his throat, and says, "I'm seventeen, alpha. Of course we can come and visit all of you once a week or so... We don't live that far from your packs..."

I smile and nod, "Yeah, we'll visit you too, since I'm sure there are many other of my female pack mates going to your pack..."

Alex grabs our attention by coughing. I laugh, and nod at him to start. He points at the girl he's holding hands with. She has long blonde curly hair, goldish blue eyes, 4'10, and was petit. She wore a pink silver lining dress, brown leather boots, silver hoop earrings, many silver and gold bracelets on both wrists, and a pink and black chocker.

"I'm Elizabeth, fifteen, and I'm from Alphas Ash's and his brothers pack... Nice to meet you, Alpha." She says in a tiny voice, and bows her head in submission.

I stare at for awhile, studying her. Then it flashes in my eyes: Them in bed naked. Then her hand on her stomach. Then her crying happily staring at two red faced babies.

I gasp, and put my hands to my head, as my whole being aches in pain, as if thousands of needles punctured me.

My mates look at me with wide eyes, and immediately hold onto me, which takes most of the pain away.

The others look at me in shock, and confusion. "Did you see it?" I look up to see my mates faces as I ask them.

They nod, and Brad replies, "Yes, since we are fully mated we saw what you were feeling, or in this case 'seeing.' But we only saw pieces..."

Conner nods, saying, "Well, I guess that's one of your first powers as a 'Pure.' I think it's when you encounter someone new, your able to either guide them to the future, or your able to see something they can't and help them understand, or know it."

"True because you did that with your Gamma's mate, Alice right?" Ash asks.

I nod in shock because I didn't know he knew that. But I look back at Elizabeth, who seems to look at me curiously. "What is it, Alpha?" She asks.

I smile at Her brightly, and ask her mischievously, "Did you mate each other yet?" She blushes, but nods. Then I look at Alex, and raise a brow at him, and ask, "Did you use protection?" He looks at me, for a moment, and then his eyes go wide, and he shakes his head no in shock.

I smile, and look at both of them, I tell them, "Well, as you can see I just saw something when I met your eyes earlier... It was of you pregnant, Elizabeth. Congrats, Alex. And, not only that, your having twins!"

Their eyes go wide, and they both look down at her stomach suspiciously. Then look at each other. They smile happily, and Alex looks at me with teary eyes, he asks, "Do you know what gender?"

I nod, but say, "I'm not telling you though because they want it a surprise. Cute twins, I'll give you a hint, but that's it... Both are the same gender."

He smiles and nods his thanks to me, then kisses his mate, and then her belly. He whispers something in her ear, and she smiles as tears fall down her face.

Everyone begins congratulating them, and hug her. I look at my mates with a huge grin on my face, and they smirk at me.

A thought pops in my head, and I look at them, and question, "How old are you guys anyways? I'm sixteen."

Ash kisses me for a quick second, and my mates in unison reply, "We just turned eighteen, a day ago.."

I smile, good, at least their still in high school. "Oh happy late birthday then. Hey, so how are we gonna do this? Do you wanna combine the pack? And where shall we move to? What are we gonna name the new pack? And what school are we gonna go to? Do we have enough houses, and a big pack house?" I ask them.

"Well, since your school is a werewolf one, we can meet halfway and buy a whole area. Cause there's a huge mansion there, and plenty of other houses. Also yeah let's combine the packs, and the name I dunno..." Brad answers.

"Oh!!! I have one!" Julie exclaimed, with a joyous smile.

"Yeah?" I ask.

"Starry Skies pack!!!" She replies instantly.

I smile and nod like everyone else does. "Okay then, we are officially Starry Skies pack, the strongest, and largest pack in the world." My mates and I say in unison, our voices echoing through out the whole floor.

I grab a knife from the table and cut my palm. I hand it to Ash who does the same, and gives it to Brad, who gives it to Conner. All four of us chant,

"To see thy love,For thy may seek,We may begin anew,From the stars above, On the centers peek,Let only us subdue,Our pack's rights,We are to sacrifice,Thy life we hold dear,With blood filled tears,We call to you, Goddess,That hence forth,To name us,Starry Skies pack!"

Then, all of us mix our blood into a wine glass and mix it. Then Conner hands it to me, and I take a drink of the blood. The guys do the same, and finish it.

People crowded around us and cheer congratulating us. I smile then kiss each of my mates, and the crowd wolf whistles at us. I blush and hug Conner, hiding my face in the crook of his neck.

I feel Brad kiss the top of my head, and Ash kiss my cheek.

I was happy to know that I had them by my side. But little did I know this was just the beginning of it all.

END OF THE PURE WOLVES!!!

Epilogue

- -

✱ Edited*Yvonne's P.O.V.

So, it's been a week since we moved into the new pack house, and neighborhood. Thank goddess, that school is only a three blocks down, so we can just walk if we wanted to.

Plus this area, has a huge forest, so us wolves can roam, and not get into trouble. Ash, Brad, Conner, and I have been getting to know each other.

I learned that Ash, loves the out doors, loves the rain, and wanted to become an environmentalist. His favorite color is blue, his favorite food is roast duck, and his favorite hobby is studying animals.

Then I learned that Brad, loves to dance, loves acting, and he says he wants to be an actor. His favorite color is yellow, his favorite food is ice cream cake, and his favorite hobby would be, and I quote, "Making love to you, babe."

Finally I learned that Conner, loves to fight, loves boxing, and he says he wants to be a detective, or an MMA fighter. His favorite color is black, his favorite food is donuts, and his favorite hobby is practicing how to shot.

I've been happy for the past week, and I know that I wouldn't have it any other way. I wish I didn't doubt them, but-

"Babe, what are you doing?" Brad asks, kissing my temple.

"Oh, just thinking. How's Elizabeth?" I reply.

"Well, ok, of course. Neva, the pack doctor, said she had about a month and a week or so to be due." Brad says.

I pull him into a kiss, playfully. He licks my lips, asking me to open. I easily open my mouth and fight him for control. He tasted of peppermint and caremel.

We brake off, I smile, and walk out into the living room. I see Elizabeth with her hands on her stomach, and Ryan has his arm around her shoulders.

I smile, and then the doors open with a start. "Alphas! Alpha Yvonne, your dad! He's collapsed!" Alex shouts as he comes running in.

We all stare at him in shock, and a tear rolls down my face.

My mates look at me in sorrow, and I run out towards the car... Driving to the hospital.

My dad, died an hour later, his final words were, "Finally... Finally, I get to see... To feel, my love again.."

He died moments later...

I cried the rest of the day. My mates just held me silently. And I fell asleep in Ash's arms.

But... if I were to know what was coming next, I would have done something that would stop the destruction.

Something.........

Anything............